RING OF HOPE

KRISTINA BECK

ISBN: 978-3-947985-16-6

NOTE TO READER

Ring Of Hope was previously published in the anthology Love Ever After. It has the same title, but has been re-edited and extended.

BOOKS BY KRISTINA BECK

Collide Series

Lives Collide

Dreams Collide

Souls Collide

Collide Series Box Set

Four Seasons Series

Snowflakes and Sapphires – Winter

Passions and Peonies – Spring

Colors and Curves – Summer

Maple Trees and Maybes – Autumn

Standalone Novels

Into Thin Air

Trapped

Key To His Heart

1

CORINNA

I prop my arms on my knees and gaze out at the glory of the rising sun. The smile on my face is as refreshing as the misty morning air.

"Remember our surfing lesson here? First and only one. The ocean was rougher than we expected, and that giant wave snuck up on us, pushing us ashore. I can still feel the slimy brown seaweed clinging to my body and the sand stuck in all the wrong places." I laugh at the memory. "I was a complete disaster. My hair, spread all over my face like a starfish, ugh. But you said I was beautiful anyway. We dragged our surfboards up the beach and collapsed on the hot sand next to them. We couldn't stop laughing."

I miss those days. It's been a while since I laughed like that.

Skimming my fingers through the golden sand around me, I enjoy the soothing sound of the waves crashing nearby. My gaze is still fixed on the purple, red, and yellow strokes painting the surrounding sky.

"You know, when I was little, I used to watch the sunrise and wonder when I'd meet my soulmate. And then I found you, and all my wishes came true. My heart was yours when you held the door open for me at my favorite bookstore. I thought nothing could beat that magical day. I was wrong." My smile fades with my voice and my eyes follow the sound of the gull, screeching as it lands about ten feet away. At least I'm not alone here anymore.

"Right here, on this beach… best day of my life. There I was, covered in seaweed and dripping wet like a fish, but you proposed. Out of the blue. We'd only been dating for six months, but I said yes without hesitation. I would've said yes even if it were only a month."

The early sun catches the glint of the platinum wedding bands on my left hand. We'd had them both engraved with our first names, our engagement date—because it's my favorite memory—and the wedding date. I remember how excited we were when we picked them up from the jeweler. One week before the wedding.

The wedding we never had.

Two years, today. My life hasn't been the same since. I wipe away the tear that trickles down my cheek. Will I ever stop crying?

Since he died, I've spent a lot of sunrises at this beach. Somehow, it's where I feel the closest to him. I don't know why, because we didn't come here often, but it's where he proposed to me, and that's my favorite memory of us.

No matter how much I ache for him, I have to stop torturing myself endlessly by coming here. It's time to move on… At least that's what my sister says, anyway. I know Liam won't walk out of the ocean and run to me; I do. But I really miss him. It's like the most important part of me died right along with him.

I need to bring myself back to life. Find that flame I used to have. But how? In the back of my mind, I think I'm waiting for a sign from him that it's okay to move on. That this gaping hole in my heart will mend. That the guilt of letting go will disappear as time goes by.

A strong gust of wind pushes against me, bringing me back to the present. I shiver and look up. Angry, gray clouds are gathering in clusters out over the Pacific. Well, that's my cue to go to work. There are brownies and other sweet surprises to be baked, along with the signature chicken salad our customers can't get enough of. I take a deep breath, pull the rings off my finger, and kiss them. Then I drop them into the black velvet pouch I store them in and slip it into my handbag. They'll be safe there until I get home.

The wind surges again, and my baseball cap lifts off my head and tumbles away from me.

Oh shit!

It's Liam's favorite one.

I jump up and run after it, but the wind is faster than I am. I must look ridiculous running after that cap, one arm stretched out in front of me, the other gripping firmly to my handbag. My long, blond hair blows all over the place, practically blinding me.

It's almost like the cap is attached to a fishing line and someone's reeling it in. There's a surfer ahead of me. It's heading his direction.

"Hey, grab my cap! Please!" I yell, waving my arms in the air. He probably can't hear me; he's a bit far away. But he looks up as if he has, drops his surfboard, and chases the cap.

He finally snags it and waves it in the air as I run up to him. Relief swims through my veins.

"Thank you so much," I say between gasps. I bend over, resting my hands on my thighs. "Man, I'm out of shape." Time to up the cardio and decrease the daily brownie intake.

"No problem," the guy says with the deepest, most velvety voice I've ever heard. It's so distinct and soothing. And familiar? How could that be?

I stand up straight and push my tangled hair away from my face. Our eyes lock, and I recognize him in an instant. His sea-green eyes are beautiful and wide with surprise.

"I know you!" We say it in unison, then laugh. He extends his hand with the cap dangling from his finger. With quick reflexes, I snatch it before it can blow away again.

Rubbing my forehead, I scramble to remember who he is. "Oh," I exclaim, snapping my fingers. "You taught my first surfing class. But that was over two years ago. Maybe I'm wrong."

His expressive eyes flash, and he nods. "Corinna, right? You're the one… Your boyfriend proposed and you said yes. Lucky man."

My smile returns because of the wonderful memory. "That's me. I'm surprised you remember that."

His mouth curls up on the side, making him look sexy as sin.

No, Liam is sexy! Was sexy!

"Not many surfing lessons end with an engagement," he explains. "Hard to forget something like that…" His voice trails off, but I could've sworn he said *or you*. My insides twist in a positive way, but I tamp down the unfamiliar emotion. He scratches his scruffy chin. "I must've been a terrible instructor—you two never came back."

I wonder what it'd feel like to brush my fingers through his disheveled, sun-kissed, sandy blond hair. It looks like he's just gotten out of the water and towel dried it, or maybe he just woke up. The unzipped wetsuit he's sporting hangs on his narrow hips, revealing a chiseled, bronzed body that you'd see in a surfer magazine.

I gulp and refuse to look below his face again, despite the bubbling hormones that beg me to do it. It's a foreign feeling that's making my pulse race. I haven't physically reacted to another man since I met Liam.

Liam! Guilt crashes through me.

Surfer dude glances over my shoulder. "I don't see your fiancé—uh, husband? Are you here alone?"

I'm caught off guard, and my face sizzles. "Yes." He

remembered my name, but not Liam's. Why? Unease sets in. I gather my hair back and put the cap on, pulling it low. I don't want him to see my face. "Um… I need to go. Thanks for your help."

"I'm sorry. Did I say something wrong?" He peers at me under the bill of my cap.

I avoid eye contact. "No. Not at all. I need to get to work."

"Oh. Okay." His dreamy voice loses its spark.

My weary eyes find their way back to him, and I freeze. His face is slack with disappointment. Does he want me to stay? It doesn't matter what he wants; I have to go. That strange, heated feeling ignites my body again, but shame isn't far behind, trying to extinguish it. I shouldn't look at him this way. He's nothing more than a stranger, even if he is a gorgeous surfer with sculpted muscles that could melt butter on an iceberg.

"Thanks for catching my hat. Don't forget your surfboard. You might need that later."

His friendly smile returns. Then I realize I'm smiling too. It's exhilarating. No, it's wrong. It's ridiculous. Ping-pong emotions are exhausting.

We head toward the abandoned board, several feet away. I should be walking in the opposite direction. "Yeah," he says. "I might need it for my next class." He winks, then glances at his watch. "Which I'm close to being late to."

"So early in the morning?"

"No better time to learn. Not a lot of people, fewer distractions." He shrugs. "I surf every morning before my lessons start. Coffee doesn't wake me up like the ocean does."

"That explains why you're already wet." I motion toward his body, and my eyes follow that movement, tracing his mouthwatering muscle definition. He grins.

"And I have a beginner's class in a few minutes. The woman needs to work, too."

Woman? My stomach clenches. Is this jealousy I'm feeling? What the hell's wrong with me this morning?

I look up at the sky, then back at him. "Even with the storm coming?"

The wind kicks up again, and a large raindrop lands on my cap. The guy's eyes grow wide, then his nose crinkles. "Um… A bird…"

I whip the cap off my head. A big glob of bird shit is splayed across it. Well, good morning to me.

He chokes back a laugh. "At least it's on your hat and not your beautiful face."

"Hilarious." I'll pretend I didn't hear him say I'm beautiful. He probably says that to all the women he talks to. I chuckle, but I want to bury myself in the sand. I run out to the water instead. He follows.

"They say it's good luck when a bird shits on you. Maybe you'll win the lottery."

I submerge the cap and shake it vigorously in the water. "I wouldn't complain."

"Listen, I'd rather stay and talk with you, but I really need to go."

My stomach twists again. It's going to be one big knot by the time I get to the café. Is he flirting with me? Doesn't he remember I should be engaged or married? A red flag springs up, but just as quickly disappears. He doesn't seem like the type to flirt with a married woman. Not that I know anything about him. The vibes he's throwing off are calm and cool.

I finish rinsing the cap, pretending I'm not talking to myself in my head. Distracted, I stand up too fast. My head spins, and I shoot out an arm to steady myself.

His large hand gently molds around my elbow. "Whoa. Are you okay?"

I close my eyes for a second to catch my bearings, then remove my arm from his grasp. The warmth from his skin lingers like it's branded my own, and I ignore my desire for it to stay there. "Y–Yes. Got up too fast."

He takes a few steps back, and I can't help but admire his solid abs as they constrict. I rub my cheek, wiping the corner of my mouth with my finger to make sure I'm not drooling.

"Well, I'll let you get to it then," I say. "It was nice seeing you again." I turn around swiftly before I can ask what his name is… or before he says something that'll make me stay. I shouldn't want to. Liam is the only man in my life.

Was the only man.

By the time I reach my car, my brain is in a fog. I rest my forehead against the steering wheel and close my eyes. The only things I see are the mesmerizing eyes from that guy who held my attention for far too long. They should be Liam's eyes I see.

Twenty minutes later, I walk through the back door of the café. The delicious scent of sweet goodness wraps around me like a baby's blanket. I'll never get sick of that smell. My sister, Annie, has already finished the second batch of our famous brownies.

"Hey, sis. Sorry I'm a few minutes late."

Rolling her shoulders, she responds, "No problem. I didn't sleep very well, so I've been here for an hour already."

I wrap my arm around her shoulder and squeeze. "Carlos just got deployed for six months. It's understandable." Sometimes I think I don't have the right to grieve anymore when I see what Annie goes through every time her husband has to leave. The difference is I wasn't prepared. Liam went to work and never returned. Annie knew the day she became an army wife she'd have to deal with Carlos's absence.

"How was the beach?" she asks, pouring melted dark chocolate into a massive bowl of flour.

I drop my arm. "A stupid bird shit on my cap. Does that answer your question?"

I am not going to tell her about surfer dude. Why didn't I

ask him what his name was? I was so wrapped up in Liam during our surfing lesson, there's no way I'd remember our instructor's name. But it's better I didn't ask. I'll never see him again. What are the chances?

Annie's laughing. "That sucks. Hey, that means good luck's around the corner, though. Maybe this place will be listed as the best café in Pismo Beach."

"Wishful thinking. Let me wash my hands, then I'll get to work."

I'll need some major distractions to forget his deep, soothing voice and chiseled perfection.

$$2$$

CORINNA

I step into my small apartment, relieved to have avoided the rain that's starting. I lock the door, then rest my aching back against it. What a day! Exhaustion kicks in and my belly's grumbling, but all I want is an ice-cold beer and a hot bath overflowing with bubbles. I toss my handbag and keys on the kitchen table and sift through it to find the pouch that holds our wedding rings. My fingers finally brush against the soft material, and I pull it out.

Instantly, I know something's wrong. My stomach clenches and my breath hitches. The pouch is too light. I yank it open and shake it upside down, waiting anxiously for two rings to fall into my hand. But only one does. With a quick glance, it's mine. I shake it again, but Liam's isn't there. My heart rate spikes so high, I think I'm going to pass out.

I dump the contents of my handbag onto the table. A tube of clear lip gloss drops down then rolls off the table, coins clink, my over-stuffed wallet thumps, and a small travel mirror bangs, landing face up. *It has to be here.* I shake the bag again and watch the other items tumble out. Tissues, pen, hairband, pack of gum, tampon, lint balls. *No ring!*

With trembling hands, I sift through the items again,

hardly able to pick the stuff up. Still no fucking ring. With a muffled cry, I swipe everything off the table in one hard swoop, watching as it all clatters and bounces against the kitchen cabinets and to the floor.

I pace back and forth, frantically checking my pants and sweatshirt pockets. Nothing.

My car!

I snag the keys off the messy floor and run outside into pouring rain. I unlock the car and lean in, searching under and between the seats, in the cupholder, the doors, even the glovebox, though I know I didn't open it. I slide the seats up and back, wishing I could rip them out. *Please. Please. Please.* No luck. I collapse into the driver's seat and pull the door shut. I pound the steering wheel until my hand pulses with pain. The car interior is soaked from the rain—or is it from my tears?

Knock, knock.

Nearly jumping out of my skin, I yelp and grab the steering wheel.

Knock, knock.

"Corinna, what are you doing in there?" Annie's muffled voice calls through the car window.

I look at her and start crying again. She whips the door open.

"What's the matter? You're drenched. Are you drunk? Is it because of what day it is?"

I jump out of the car and grab her shoulders. "Omigod, Annie! I can't find it."

She pulls away, keeping the umbrella over us. "You can't find what? Your keys?"

"No!" I wail, wiping my nose with the back of my hand. "Liam's wedding band. It wasn't in my bag when I got home. I had it this morning. I've been searching the car—" Inspiration strikes, and I catch my breath. "Wait! Maybe it's at the café."

I turn to jump back in the car, but Annie stops me. "Give me the keys. I'll drive you. We'll find it!"

Two hours later, we walk through my apartment door, empty-handed. It wasn't at the café either. I wanted to go search the beach, but Annie convinced me it was too dark and stormy to do that tonight. Helplessness and exhaustion floods over me.

She helps me straighten up the kitchen, and when we're done, I plop down onto a wooden chair. Annie pulls two beers out of the fridge, pops the caps, then hands one to me.

I take a long swig. "Thanks for helping. It was nice to have someone there with me…" Tears fill my eyes again. "What am I gonna do, Annie? What if I don't find it? You know how important that ring is to me." My head pounds.

My sister rubs my shoulders comfortingly. "We'll go to the beach tomorrow before we open. If we don't find it, I'll go on that Facebook page for lost-and-found items in our area. Maybe somebody's found it. Hey, let's check now."

She's got her phone out and is pulling up the community page when suddenly it hits me. *The guy from today.* Guilt doubles, triples. I leap from my chair. "Fuck! That's it," I yell. "I'm being punished! That's why this happened!"

She freezes, her eyes wide. "Corinna, what the hell are you talking about? Please, sit back down." She pulls the chair closer and urges me toward it. "You're freaking me the hell out."

"There was a guy at the beach today, and I noticed how attractive he was. I wasn't looking, I swear. Guys are never on my radar because Liam will always be the one for me." I sit down for a second, then pop back up. "And get this! He was our surf instructor the day Liam proposed. He remembered us and my name. The guy asked where Liam was, and I didn't have the heart to tell him he'd died. I tried to walk away, but that's when the bird shit on me." I'm babbling frantically, and I know it. I pull on my shirt collar, trying to calm myself.

Annie puts an arm around my shoulders, stopping me from pacing the kitchen floor. "There is absolutely nothing wrong with talking to another man." I shrug, and she huffs with exasperation. "Listen to me!"

"But it wasn't just talking! There was a connection between us. A zing. Whatever you want to call it. Almost like when I was with Liam." I drop onto the chair again and cover my face. "His voice just… sucked me in and made me want to stay with him. That shouldn't have happened. Did I cheat on Liam by noticing how beautiful this guy's green eyes were or how sexy he looked with his wetsuit hanging off his hips?"

I squeeze my eyes shut as the image of him forms in my mind again. Goosebumps cover my body, but my face heats up.

Annie massages her temples. "Corinna, you're overanalyzing again, like you do with everything. Did you get his name?"

"No. I didn't remember it and it felt too personal to ask. Like I'd open up a door to let him in my heart."

"Seriously?" Her voice borders on disbelief or derision. "This is fucking nuts, Corinna. I know you don't want to hear this, but Liam has been dead for two years! Just because you *finally* noticed a good-looking guy doesn't mean you cheated on him. He would want you to move on and find someone to make you happy again."

"I am happy… Sort of."

"Sometimes, yeah. But I see when you get lost in your thoughts and when your mood changes. It's okay to be unhappy and still grieving, but it's almost like you think you're not allowed to enjoy life. If you were the one who had died, would you want Liam to never find happiness again?"

I remain silent, trying to digest what she's saying. "It'd kill me to see him with someone else, but he's a man you couldn't help loving. He'd deserve to be loved and appreciated for the great man he is. Or was."

"So why aren't you allowed to find love again? Or just freakin' go on a date with someone? Being attracted to a man proves you aren't numb anymore. You're only twenty-eight and you have a long life ahead of you. Liam will always be in your heart, but that's all. You need to find what can make you happy now. And I'm not just talking about men."

"I can't imagine loving someone as much as I loved… *love* Liam."

That can only happen once. Right?

3

CLAY

"Hey, Mom," I say, kissing her forehead.

"Hi, sweetie," she replies, patting my hand that's resting on her shoulder.

"Find anything valuable at the beach today?" I peek at the couple of items on the table in front of her.

"Not much," she grumbles. "Just a couple of quarters and some screws. There are days when I hit the jackpot and others when it's slim pickings. Oh, it doesn't matter anyway. You know I just do it for fun. It keeps me busy."

Dad died a year ago, and ever since, Mom can't seem to be still. Dad had multiple sclerosis and died of a lung infection. His sickness kept her running all the time. Now she works part-time at a doctor's office. Her downtime includes Pilates and daily beach searches with a metal detector. She's found all kinds of things, ranging from dirty silverware to a Rolex watch and several cell phones. The other day, she brought home a beautiful gold necklace with a heart charm. She posts all her findings in a Facebook group for lost-and-found items in Pismo Beach, California. Her Facebook name, Treasure Hunter, is well known because she's made so many people happy. A few times, she's even received a cash reward.

I take a seat on the bench next to the worktable where she's cleaning her findings from the day. "Has anyone responded to your post about the necklace yet?"

She shakes her head. "Not since I looked last. You know it can take several days. Anyway, enough about me. How are you doing in your new townhouse? Have you unpacked everything?"

"Only a couple of boxes left. I love the ocean view and not having to drive to work anymore. I'm spoiled."

"You've worked hard; you deserve it. Have you gone to that cute little restaurant I told you about, Sunshine Café? The brownies are to die for, and the chicken salad sandwich is the best." She kisses her fingers with a flourish. "I could drink their coffee all day long, too. You know how picky I am with coffee. When's your next day off? I could stop by and see how your place looks, and then I'll introduce you to the café to celebrate your new home and the success of your surfing school."

I take my phone out of my pocket and scan my calendar. "Tomorrow's a quiet day. I don't have any classes until late afternoon. If you have time, I could do breakfast or lunch."

"Late lunch sounds good because I have to work in the morning. I'll walk the beaches when you go to work."

"Sounds like a plan," I say, adding it to my calendar. "Hey, do you remember the story I told you about a couple who got engaged during one of my lessons when I worked at Surf and Learn?"

"Vaguely," she mumbles while shining a quarter like it's a diamond. "Why?"

I shrug. "No reason, really. Just, I saw the woman at the beach yesterday."

She peers at me over the rim of her glasses. "You did? How do you know it was her?"

"I'd recognize her anywhere." I grin replaying our conversation in my head.

She sets the quarter down and places her glasses on the table. "Oh, really?" She draws out the word, a knowing smile on her face. Figures, I mention a woman and that's when she gives me her full attention.

"Now, don't get excited." I laugh with my hands up. "The wind blew her baseball cap off and it flew right toward me. So I caught it."

It was strange, though. Almost like it was meant to happen. I mean, we were the only two people on the beach. That hat could have blown anywhere.

Her eyebrow tips up on one side, knowing there's more. "Did she recognize you?"

"Surprisingly, yes. When I asked her where her fiancé was —probably her husband now—her eyes lost their sparkle and she wanted to leave. But then, before she could go, a bird shit on her cap. It's selfish to say, but I've never been more thankful. I got to talk to her for a few minutes more. Long enough to see she wasn't wearing a ring."

"Hmm. Did you remember her name?"

"At first, no. I was too blinded by her beauty to focus on anything else." *I sound like such a sap.* "Then it came back to me. Corinna."

She's an illusion! I've been telling myself that all day, but I've thought about this woman so many times since that lesson, always kind of hoping to get a glimpse of her angelic face and bright blue eyes. My memory didn't do her justice, though. Not even close.

"Pretty name," Mom says, reaching across the table for a clean hand towel.

"It fits her. Gorgeous long, blond hair, eyes that put you in a trance, and a smile that could turn any grouch into a cheerleader." I comb my hand through my hair, wondering why I'm saying all this aloud.

Mom leans forward. "And you're frustrated *because*?"

I laugh and shake my head. "Because I'm so damn jealous of the man she got engaged to. I wished it was me that day, not him. And today? He wasn't there, but I let her walk away again. I should've at least found out why she was alone."

But I didn't.

4

CORINNA

First thing I did when I woke up this morning was check the Facebook post Annie made about Liam's ring. We combed the beach for more than an hour yesterday and found nothing. I can't stop crying about it.

Some people might think I'm foolish for getting upset over losing a piece of metal, but I can't help it. That ring connects my soul to his. Without it, the hole in my heart is even bigger. It feels like I've lost him all over again. Well, not quite, but it still hurts like a bitch.

But I suppose life goes on… like it always does. Time to make the brownies.

Annie's busy washing a silver bowl at the café when I arrive. I'm beginning to think, with Carlos deployed, she might be living here. I walk in, put my things in the back, and grab a clean apron.

"Morning," I mumble.

"Hey there," Annie responds, wiping her hands on a dish towel. She walks around the counter and rubs my arm. "How are you holding up?"

I sigh, casting my eyes away from hers. "I checked Facebook again and nothing."

"Be patient and have some faith," she urges, clasping my hand. "It's only been two days."

"*Pfft.* Easy for you to say. I've been running low on faith for the last two years." Annie's jaw clenches, lets my hand go, and her eyes turn bitter. I drop my chin to my chest. "I'm sorry for being such a downer." Negativity blurts from my mouth without me realizing it most of the time. With one glimpse of Annie's stern face, I know when to shut up.

She breaks the silence by saying, "Do you want to work in the front to get your mind off things? You can send Caitlin back here. She can help me."

Tying the apron behind my back, I shrug. "That's not a bad idea." Once the knot is secure, I embrace her. "Thanks for being the best sister anyone could have. I'd be lost without you."

She pulls away and smirks. "I agree... I am the best. Now go to the front and socialize with our customers. And that means smile. We want them to come back. We *need* them to if we want to stay open."

I put on the standard Sunshine Café owner's smile and get to work.

After a busy morning and lunch, I wipe down the counters and the espresso machine until they're sparkling. My mouth's parched from talking so much. There are no customers at the counter, so I run to the back for my water bottle. As I approach the front again, I hear that familiar deep, velvety voice and my heart skips a beat... or two.

It's the surfer! He's here. *Shit! What do I do?* I duck down, hoping no one can see me.

"Why are you hiding behind the espresso machine?" Annie surprises me from behind. "It better be good since there are two people waiting at the counter."

"*Shh!* I know." She bends at her knees so we're eye to eye. "I just needed a sip of water."

"Hunched down on the floor? I could maybe understand

if you were shoving a brownie in your mouth." She eyes me with suspicion, stands up slowly, then looks toward the front counter.

"Whoever the guy is standing there, he's a hottie, but don't tell Carlos I said that." She giggles, then nudges me with her knee to get my act together. "Go take his order."

I stand up and see his profile because he's looking at the menu on the wall. My stomach is in knots. Good knots at first, but then the guilt tries to worm its way in. *Nope. Not gonna happen this time.*

He looks in my direction, and his face lights up. I can't see my own face, but I'm pretty sure it mirrors his at this moment. A gorgeous smile like his is contagious.

"Wow. This is a surprise. We run into each other two times within a few days," he exclaims. My cheeks sizzle, and my insides quiver like a scared rabbit.

"Hi. Welcome to my café. Well, mine and my sister's." I glance at the beautiful, grinning woman next to him. She's been here before. Maybe his mom?

She extends her hand to me. "I'm Bev Anderson, Clay's mom. I adore this place."

Clay Anderson.

She nudges his arm with her elbow. "And you are?" She glances at my name tag, and her eyes flash. "Corinna. What a pretty name."

My smile broadens. "Corinna Banks, and thanks. Nice to meet you. I've seen you here before. I'm usually in the back, though."

"So how do you and Clay know each other?" Bev's curious eyes volley between me and Clay.

"Well, um." I wipe my sweaty hands on my coffee-stained apron. *Attractive, Corinna.* And I can only imagine what my hair looks like.

Why does he make me so damn nervous?

"I saw him at the beach two days ago."

He chimes in and explains how we met in the past. I can't keep my eyes off him or stop myself from melting when I hear him speak. His mom nods with a sweet smile.

"I just moved into a townhouse a couple blocks from here," he says to me. "My mom loves your brownies and sandwiches. She's been begging me to come here for lunch. I'm glad I agreed."

Me too.

Someone clears their throat. Entranced by their presence, I haven't noticed the line behind them. I rattle my head to come out of my stupor. "Would you like to order something? I don't mean to rush you, but there's a line forming."

Clay glances behind him, then back to me. "Oops. Sorry. You can order for us, Mom."

"Let's see. Um, two brownies, two chicken salad sandwiches, one cappuccino, and one glass of water, please," Bev says.

"For here or to go?"

Please say you'll stay.

"Here," he says instantly. His friendly eyes hold my gaze, making my heart flutter. I shouldn't feel this way, but it's almost out of my control. I push the bad thoughts back into the dark where they belong.

"Great. I'll bring your order when it's ready. Take any table you'd like."

He pays, then they walk off.

As if Caitlin can read my mind, she comes out from the back.

"Caitlin, please take over the front again. I need to prepare an order." She nods and helps the next customer.

I dash to the back to tell Annie.

She looks up and wipes vanilla icing off her chin. I guess my face says it all. "What's the matter now? You look like you saw an alien."

"Definitely not an alien. Remember the guy I saw at the beach?" I whisper, peeking over my shoulder.

Her eyes spring open and she nods.

I jut my chin toward the front of the café.

"He's here? Now?"

I nod with wide eyes.

"Did he recognize you?"

I nod again because I can't find my tongue.

"Let me see. Does he want a coffee?"

"They ordered a cappuccino and a water."

"What does he look like?"

"He's the guy at the counter who you said was hot!" I slap my hand over my mouth. That came out way too loud.

"Oh. This should be fun," Annie says, wiggling her eyebrows. I roll my eyes. Nonchalantly, she walks out to the front where she prepares the cappuccino. I follow her, then grab plates and take out two brownies from the case.

On her tiptoes, she scans the room, then zones in on the corner table near the front window. Slowly, she lowers to her heels and places the steaming cup on a tray. I hand her a glass of ice water and look at her pleadingly.

"Could you take this to them while I make the sandwiches?"

She flashes me a mischievous grin. "No problem. I want to see him up close and personal. Maybe get to know this mystery man."

"Hey! Don't embarrass me," I warn, "or you'll have to clean the kitchen by yourself when we close!"

She rests her hand on her chest. "Now why would I embarrass you?"

"Because you love to do it any chance you get."

"That's what sisters do," she teases. "Don't worry. I just want to meet the guy my sister's crushing on. That doesn't happen every day."

"I don't have a crush. It's just a zing."

She rolls her eyes. "Same thing."

I can't quite straighten the grin on my own face.

Annie picks up the tray. "Excuse me. I have work to do. Go prepare their sandwiches and do some breathing exercises to calm down. He's a cute guy, that's all. Don't make it so complicated."

I grin, but it fades quickly as she turns. *But it is complicated.* Remorse knocks on the door, and I remember how I lost Liam's ring... And him. *Just let me have this bit of excitement.*

I scurry to the kitchen to prepare the rest of their order. I can't witness this. It takes a few minutes to get their food ready, and by that time I've mellowed out a bit. Annie hasn't come back, so I'm sure she's chatting away like she usually does. She loves interacting with the customers. I take a deep breath and hope for the best.

Annie's infectious laughter fills the air as I walk around the counter. Who knows what story she's telling when her arms are waving about like that. Clay and Bev laugh along with her. Once I'm at the table, I slide the plates in front of them.

"Thanks. This looks delicious," Clay says and Bev agrees with him.

"You're welcome." I flip the tray under my arm and say to Annie, "So, what were you telling our customers that's so funny?"

"Just telling them when I discovered I wanted to open a café."

"When you dropped a full tray of food on a customer's lap... one or two jobs ago." I shake my head. "Nothing to brag about."

"Hey. I'm a perfectionist. It made me want to be the best. Look at where we are today." She spreads her arms out to show off our beautiful café.

"When I started surfing at twelve years old, I was horrible," Clay chimes in.

"He really was." Bev chuckles.

Clay squints his eyes, but can't hold back a smile. "Mom, let's not go there. Anyway, I had an excellent trainer who always told me not to give up and to keep pushing myself to be better. I ended up loving it and realized I was pretty good after a while."

"*Pfft.* Pretty good." Bev shakes her head. "He's won a fair share of surfing championships." She leans toward us and hides behind her hand. "He doesn't like to talk about it."

I glance at him and watch as his cheeks turn a soft shade of pink. Adorable *and* modest.

"Wow. How cool!" Annie says enthusiastically, raising her hand like she's holding a glass of wine. "To never giving up."

"I'll drink to that," Clay says, raising his water. Our eyes catch again. "Never give up."

"Never give up," I repeat, nodding slightly. The phrase has its own meaning for me, but the way he's looking at me… It's like he's trying to tell me something, but he can't possibly know what I've been through.

Annie's oblivious, thankfully, and she babbles on. "Clay told me where he gives lessons. Remember that store on the beach that used to rent bikes?"

It takes a few seconds to picture it, then I nod.

"He took it over and turned it into a surfing school." *Impressive.* "He has a late afternoon class scheduled today. Why don't we go watch after we close up? I could use some fresh ocean air after being in here all day. Isn't there a tiki bar nearby? We deserve a drink or two."

Clay waves his hand. "Wait a second. You don't have to do that. Watching me teach is hardly the most exciting thing you could do."

It is if you'll be in that wetsuit again.

"Of course it is," Bev says proudly. "I love watching you." She turns to us. "I think you should."

Pressure much?

But I am a little curious about how well he surfs. I didn't exactly notice Clay when Liam and I had our lesson. *Oh, shit.* They're all looking at me.

"Um. Yeah. Sure. I have nothing planned."

I'm going to kill Annie.

5

CLAY

"I can't believe you two did that!" I let the door close behind us before I speak, but I have to say it. With Corinna's wide eyes and blotchy neck, I know I wasn't the only one uncomfortable being put on the spot like that. "You do remember I'm thirty, right? I don't need my mom to fix me up with a girl!" I'm not mad, but I am embarrassed. For Corinna and me.

"Sorry, dear. I know I got a little carried away in there." Mom stops by her car and opens the trunk. She looks at me thoughtfully, then reaches in for a bag, small shovel, and her metal detector. I take the detector from her and lean it against the car. She drops the shovel in the bag and gives me her full attention again. "I don't care what you say, Clay. That girl likes you. There's something holding her back—some sort of sadness. But her whole being brightened when she saw you. And that's important."

When Corinna greeted us with a stunning smile as if she were as happy to see me as I was her, my stomach did a backflip and adrenaline coursed through my veins. If I'd known she was the owner of this café, I would've been here days ago. She probably would have had to kick me out because I wouldn't have left without her agreeing to a date with me. But now I know, and my pulse quickens again.

"Well, thanks for playing stupid and not letting on that I'd already told you I'd seen her on the beach." I shut the trunk for her, then pick up the detector, and we amble over to the boardwalk.

"I'm your mother. Your face said it all. It was obvious you didn't want me to say anything."

"And what do you see now?" When we step on the boardwalk, I stop and turn to her. She does the same.

"That you've got it bad for this woman." Mom pauses, takes a breath. "Corinna's quite beautiful, Clay. But you have to tread lightly and somehow find out why she has a wall up. She's fragile and protecting herself like she's had her heart broken. My gut tells me she never got married."

Yeah, mine too. "I don't think Annie would've suggested watching my lesson if she were. And Corinna wasn't wearing a ring today either. I'll see what happens if they stop by later. I don't want to come off like an asshole for trying to date a married woman, but… if she's single, maybe I'll ask her to have a drink with me."

We walk along the beach, until Mom stops almost exactly where I ran into Corinna. I keep that fact to myself, but it's kind of funny that she's picked this spot to search today. So many coincidences.

She gives me a quick hug. "Okay, son," she says. "Go to work. I have a lot of sand to search through. Hopefully, I'll find something interesting today—not just a set of keys or a damn lighter again. Call me tomorrow and let me know how it went."

"Will do. Good luck." I hug her back, then continue along the water toward my shop. A swirl of nerves and excitement has my concentration shot to shit. All I can think about is whether Corinna will show up. Surfing will be the best cure for that.

A couple hours later, I'm waiting for my student. The waves are perfect for a surfer of his level. The temperature is cooler than usual, which I love. And there's a promise for a spectacular sunset.

"Hey, Clay. I'm stoked. The waves are awesome today." My twenty-year-old student, Toby, has arrived. He stands next to me with his bright yellow board and a lopsided grin.

"How's it going?" We bump fists after he leans the board on the wooden railing. "I hope that means you've been practicing. The winds are inshore today. It could get a little rough out there. You up for that?"

"Bet your ass. I can't let an old fart like you be better than me for much longer."

I punch his arm. "I'll show you old fart, smartass. We'll come back to this topic the day you get barreled."

He throws his head back and laughs. "You need to work out. You punch like a little girl with pigtails."

"Whatever." I snicker. "So where's Mariah? Bored of watching you fall off your board?"

Toby flips me the bird. "Aw. Are you jealous I have a girl-friend?" he jabs, wiggling his eyebrows.

Very jealous. I'm not into casual hookups or the bar scene anymore, and meeting Corinna again made me realize how lonely I've been. It'd be nice to share my time with someone other than my clients and married friends.

"She had to work. You shouldn't be wondering about my relationship. When are you going to start dating someone?"

"Hi, Clay." Toby and I turn toward the familiar, soft voice. My heart leaps out of my chest and runs to Corinna to say hi to hers.

"Speaking of date," Toby mutters under his breath. My hand smacks him in the gut. "*Oof.* Such abuse."

Annie and Corinna watch us, grinning. I saunter over to them. "Hello, ladies. Glad you came. I wasn't sure if you were just being nice."

"And miss eye candy on surfboards and drinks on the beach? Are you crazy?" Annie remarks with a gleam in her eyes.

Corinna stands next to her laughing, looking even more beautiful than ever. Her corn-silk blond hair is pulled over her left shoulder in a loose braid. A few strands have escaped and blow freely in the breeze. Her glossy lips shimmer in the sunshine. The form-fitting sundress she's wearing enhances her mouthwatering curves and matches the color of her sparkling bright blue eyes—the same eyes that are sucking in every inch of my torso, leaving a trail of heat on my skin that's hotter than the sun. *Wow.* The seawater had better be really cold to keep certain body parts under control.

From the moment I met her that first day, I knew she was the one for me, but circumstances and timing weren't on my side. Now, I have another chance. I think.

Patience. I need patience.

"You're just in time. Toby and I were about to start. He has a thirty-minute lesson. Are you going to sit at the tiki bar?"

Corinna glances at Annie. Annie nods.

"Yes. There's an excellent view from there. When you're done, come find us," Corinna suggests, then scopes me out again with flames in her eyes. I didn't expect that when the others could've easily noticed. *Game on.*

"Cool. Enjoy the view." I aim that comment only to her, then turn away. "Come on, Toby. Let's show them what you can do." We zip up our suits and grab our boards.

Half an hour later, we jog out of the water. "That was your best day yet, man." I pat his shoulder. "Good job."

"The waves kicked my ass, but I love it." We trot over to the office, lean our boards against the wooden railing again, and grab towels.

Toby clears his throat and mumbles into his hand, "Your girlfriend's coming. Behind you."

"She's only a friend," I whisper through clenched teeth, unzipping my wetsuit.

"Denial. See you next week," he says, waving as he walks away. I let out a soft laugh while peeling the clinging suit off my upper body.

I turn around to find Corinna approaching me alone. She halts, then rubs the back of her neck.

"Hi. I hope that wasn't too boring for you." I dry my face, then my pecs. She doesn't respond as her gaze lingers on my chest. I chuckle to myself and repeat what I said.

"Oh! Not at all. You look—I mean, you *were* amazing. Do you still compete?" Her eyes finally focus on my face. "You make it look so easy."

"I stopped about four years ago. My body had enough. Teaching's the next best thing." Scanning the people around us, I ask, "Where's Annie? Still at the bar?"

Corinna stands near my board and grasps the handbag strap hanging off her shoulder. "She had to go. I came over to say good night."

I deflate with disappointment. "Do you really have to go? I'm finished for the day and it's still early."

"I should—I need to. Maybe some other time." She turns to leave.

Nope. I'm not letting her get away. I take a chance and step in front of her, almost bumping our heads. "Come on. I'm starving—I always am after surfing. Want to go for a bite to eat? Just food. Nothing else." I need to put her at ease. If she thinks I'm asking her on a date—which I kind of am—she might run.

She glances around and then at her feet. "Um."

I should say forget it. The last thing I want to do is pressure or scare her. If she doesn't want to spend time with me, I don't want her to. But I can't give up.

Corinna's eyes connect with mine and suddenly her sexy lips tug up at the corners, and her wall begins to crumble.

Well, not all of it, but it's a start. It's amazing how a genuine smile can transform her face.

"Sure," she finally says. "I'm hungry, too. I love the brownies we bake, but I can only eat so many. Where do you want to go?"

Relief and excitement release the tension from my shoulders and neck. "Do you like tacos?"

"Of course. Who doesn't?" She chuckles. I love the soft sound; I want to hear it on repeat. From the way she acts, I don't think she laughs often.

"Good answer. Ever been to Tacos Galore?"

Her eyebrows pinch together and, for an instant, her body freezes like a statue. Then she reaches up to play with the delicate gold chain around her neck. I can practically see the bricks stacking themselves back up with every second that passes.

What the hell did I say?

Suddenly she relaxes. Whatever internal battle was raging, she apparently won. "I love Tacos Galore," she says. "I haven't been there in a while. Let's go."

Phew. "Okay, great. Give me fifteen minutes to clean up. Do you want to wait in my office or relax in a sunchair out here? Whatever you do, just don't run off." This is one of those moments I'm glad I had a proper hot water shower installed outside. No need to run home to get ready when everything I need is right here. What I should really be doing is closing the office for the night. The list of things I need to do can wait until after she leaves.

"I'll sit out here. Don't worry. I'm not going anywhere." A faint smile graces her perfect face, assuring me.

Don't think I won't be fisting the air once I'm in the shower.

6
─────

CORINNA

Once he's out of sight, I slap my hand on my forehead and begin to pace. What the hell am I doing? And why did I agree to go with him to Liam's favorite restaurant, of all places?

Annie! It's her fault. But it's mine, too. I want to spend time with Clay. I can't avoid places just because Liam and I used to go there. A lot of things remind me of Liam, but that doesn't mean I should be miserable. *That's right!* The smug little voice in my head sounded almost exactly like Annie.

I stop in front of a chair and realize I'm too antsy to sit. My brain won't stop spinning. Watching Clay surf was a hell a lot better than sitting home alone. Some of those waves were high and rough, but he rode them like it was child's play. His student was pretty good too. Every time a big wave was on their tails, Annie and I would cheer them on. The adrenaline high was a great distraction.

I haven't been able to stop admiring Clay's perfect, muscular body since I got here. That gorgeous smile that grew on his face when he saw me… speechless! A man hasn't smiled at me like that since Liam. Then again, I haven't been looking.

Ugh! Annie's right. I always go back to Liam. She got frustrated with me when we were at the tiki bar. No matter what she said about Clay, I compared him to Liam. She said I wasn't giving Clay a fair chance. Will I do this with any guy that shows interest in me?

Maybe… Probably… Yes.

But I can change that right now. I hear some movement behind me and turn around. Clay steps out of his office freshly showered and locks the door.

"Okay. I'm ready. Want to walk?" Damn! He looks just as divine in the khaki shorts and white linen shirt he's wearing as he did in that wetsuit. This outfit shows off his surfer tan and bright eyes.

"Sure. I don't mind. That means I can eat more tacos."

"Let's see who can eat the most. How about we make a bet?" He walks backward in front of me so he's facing me. His adorable grin stretches ear to ear.

I cock an eyebrow. "You sure you want to do that? I'm known as the Taco Queen."

"I'm always up for a challenge. My appetite is ferocious right now. If I eat more than you, you have to take another surfing lesson. How about that? Maybe you'll enjoy it this time."

I chuckle. "Who said I didn't the first time?"

"Well, you never came back."

"Maybe I went somewhere else." I stick my nose in the air, teasing him.

"Don't give me that." He peeks over his shoulder to make sure he won't bump into something or trip on the boardwalk. "Anyway, do we have a deal?"

I prop my hands on my hips. "Hmm. We'll see. Let me think of something you'll have to do if I win."

Maybe it'll involve his lips kissing mine.

~

We walk out of the restaurant… or more like roll out of it. My belly hurts both from eating and from laughing too much. Our casual conversation was pure, innocent fun.

Clay bumps his shoulder against mine lightly. "Taco Queen, you are. Where does a woman with your slender waist hide all those tacos you've just eaten? I'm in awe. Should I bow, your majesty?"

"Don't make me laugh again. I'm ready to burst," I say, bumping him back. "I might regret it tomorrow, or even in a couple of hours. Thank God we walked here." I'm also buzzed from the couple of beers I drank.

We stroll toward the boardwalk that leads us to his office.

"Thanks for coming with me. Maybe we can do it again some time," Clay says casually. "I had a lot of fun."

"Me, too. I haven't relaxed like this in a while. Annie and I are always busy with the café. You're the first guy I've gone to dinner with since—"

Damn! Have I mentioned that I talk too much when I drink?

He places his hand softly on my arm. We stop walking. "Since what?"

I shake my head and wave it off. "Never mind. Let's keep going."

Clay opens his mouth to say something but purses his lips instead.

We continue in comfortable silence for seconds or maybe minutes. Quicker than expected, it's time to say goodbye. Half of my broken heart begs for me to stay with Clay, and the other part wants me to disappear.

He puts his hand on the small of my back. "Before we call it a night, let's sit in the sand and watch the rest of the sunset. It's too beautiful not to."

What's a couple more minutes? When's the last time I watched the sunset? Or enjoyed anything? I'm like a robot —I go to work numb, day in and day out. I hide my emotions behind the counter, then go home to an empty apartment.

"So, what do you say?" His gentle voice interrupts my deep thoughts.

"Um, sure. It's been a while since I've watched the sunset." He guides me forward, but I stop again. "Wait. I want to take off my shoes."

He does the same, then we meander toward the water. My heart urges me to find his hand. Shocked, I clasp both hands behind my back instead.

"How about here?" Clay asks.

I glance behind us to check how far we've walked. Then I plop down because I'm tired. He follows.

I cross my legs at the ankles and lean back on my hands. "I live so close to the ocean, but I don't appreciate it enough."

"Mmm, this is my favorite part of the day. After I finish up at the office, I relax on the beach or my balcony at home. It's so peaceful."

Taking a deep breath, I enjoy the salty smell of the sea breeze and a hint of Clay's citrusy cologne. His heavenly scent wraps itself around me, filling my body with warmth and peace. Or it's the beer.

Nah, it's him.

"I know I lost the taco bet, but maybe you can try surfing again, anyway?" My back stiffens in response. "It's a great workout. Not that I'm saying you need— I mean— You're perfect the way you are." His voice peters out.

Ignoring his compliment, I say, "No thanks. I don't think I'll ever surf again."

"Why?"

I don't answer.

"Please tell me. I know you're dealing with something, and I have so many questions. Like why are you here with me when I saw you get engaged a couple years ago?

I jump up, stumble, and catch myself before I fall back on

my ass. "I don't have to answer that. I need to go." I grab my shoes and turn to leave.

Get a grip, Corinna! Stop running—from your life and Clay.

He jumps up just as quickly. "Not yet. Please stay and talk to me. I know there's something between us. We hardly know each other, but I'm so drawn to you. I think you feel it, too, but you're scared. Why? Did he hurt you?"

Tears prickle behind my eyes. "Yes, but not in the way you think."

"I don't get it, Corinna." He steps closer to me and rubs my arm gently. I don't pull away. "Please explain it to me. Maybe it'll help."

I waver back and forth, then give in. "When I met Liam, it was love at first sight. For him too. We were only together a short time before we got engaged. We set the wedding date for three months later. I wish we'd have eloped." Sorrow drips from every part of my body.

Even though I'm talking about another man, Clay listens intently. His sympathetic eyes and slight nod of his head encourages me to keep going.

"Liam was an electrician. There was an accident at the construction site where he was working. He was electrocuted and died instantly. Instead of a wedding, we had a funeral. You saw me on the beach the other day because it was two years since he'd died. I feel closest to him there, where we got engaged."

Clay wipes the tears from my cheeks and pulls me into his arms. He hugs me tightly and lets me cry. My shoes slip from my grasp and I wrap my arms around him, releasing a contented sigh.

He whispers in my ear, "I'm sorry, Corinna. You're so young and have already suffered so much. I wish I could take away your pain."

I rest my hands on his hips and sink into him. "You're doing more than you know. It feels good to be held like this. I try not to show my grief anymore, but it sneaks out. Annie gets the brunt of it."

"You're lucky to have her." I nod in agreement.

I let myself enjoy his comforting embrace for another minute, then reluctantly break our connection. We're still close enough that I can see the colorful sky reflect in his intense eyes. His full pink lips entice me to kiss them.

He cups my face with his hands. "Corinna, give me a chance to make you happy again. From the moment I saw you the first time, I haven't forgotten you. I know that sounds… crazy, but it's true. My heart raced more than on the best wave I've ever ridden. But then Liam walked up behind you and wrapped his arms around your waist. The way you looked at him over your shoulder, and the way he kissed you on the cheek… I wanted to be him. For you to smile at me like that. And when I saw you earlier this week— it all came flooding back."

"I— I don't know what to say." I was so oblivious. Still am. My love for Liam was blinding then, and it's holding me back now.

A soft smile transforms his face. "You two were so in love, it was obvious. And then, you got engaged right here on the beach, and my heart cracked open because I knew I'd never have a chance to be with you.

"Then your baseball cap came flying right at me. And then your café… I don't think any of this was mere coincidence. I haven't been seriously involved with anyone since then because no one has ever made my heart light up like that. Not until I saw you the other day. My soul recognized yours then, but knew you weren't mine to have. Not yet anyway."

He takes my hand and lays it flat on his chest. "Do you feel my heart pounding? This is what you do to me. My blood is on fire when you're next to me. I can't keep my eyes off you. I know you're still hurting, but can you give me a chance? You might have been in love before, but I've never been. With you, I could be."

My breath catches in my throat because of how beautiful and desirable he makes me feel. It's different from Liam, but in a good way. Maybe it's because I've changed. I'm not the same person I was back then.

Clay's gaze caresses my face, making me blush. He releases my hand and brushes my cheek with his thumb. Shivers of delight travel up and down my spine. The air charges around us.

"Please let me kiss you. Even if it's only once," he pleads.

His tempting lips are dangerously close to mine. My heart thunders with anticipation.

His eyes ask for permission, and I nod.

Clay wraps an arm around my lower back. I close my eyes and part my lips as he lowers his mouth to mine. His soft lips brush against them gently, and my pulse spikes from this simple touch. I drag my hands down his solid chest, then grip his shirt, and pull him flush against me. His mouth crashes on to mine, and I open for him. His tongue sweeps in, and with one sweet taste of him, my control snaps. Raw need mixes with pure desire. We kiss with desperation as I wrap my arms around his neck.

He traces his fingers along the sides of my breasts making me shudder. A sound I don't recognize escapes me. My hands travel down his solid back and land on his firm ass, giving it a gentle squeeze. His hard length presses against my stomach. Moans escape both of us. This is unreal.

"You taste better than I could've imagined. I could kiss you all night. Let me," Clay whispers, pressing petal soft kisses down my neck, focusing on my racing pulse. I lean my head to the side to encourage him to keep going.

What is he doing to me? I'm stuck in a haze that surrounds me. The flame that I thought I had lost is now a burning inferno. I want more. All that he can give me. Am I dreaming? Because this is amazing… He's amazing.

Too amazing.

My eyes spring open. I break away, covering my mouth that tastes deliciously like him. I shouldn't like it. Liam is the only one I love.

"I'm so sorry, Clay. This shouldn't have happened. I can't do this."

"Wait. Don't go," he says, trying to grab my hand.

I run away as fast as I can, confused as all hell. He calls my name in the distance, but I ignore him.

Just when I think he's given up, I hear him call my name again, and he's right behind me.

"Corinna, please stop," he says with gutted sadness. "Please."

I do, but don't turn around.

"You forgot your shoes. You can't go home barefoot." He places them on the sand next to me. A few seconds pass in silence. He sighs. "Fine. You might regret what just happened, but I never will. Good-bye, Corinna."

Good-bye sounds final. I shouldn't let him walk away. And I shouldn't either.

But I do.

Because I'm a complete fool, living in the past.

I couldn't sleep last night, so here I am at the café at the crack of dawn. I needed to get out of my apartment. Annie isn't even here yet. She called last night, but I didn't have the energy to explain what I'd done to Clay. *With* Clay. I texted her instead, told her I'd talk to her in the morning.

Then I sat in my living room and looked through all the photos I have of Liam and me. We had planned to make a photobook each year so we could look back at them when we are old—to remember all the good times we had together. We didn't even get a year.

It hit me hard and made me realize that… it's time. I need to finally donate his clothes still hanging in my closet. Throw out the half-empty bottle of his cologne on the bathroom sink. Do something with his hardly used golf clubs. Maybe his parents will want some stuff. It's been months since the last time I spoke to them.

It's time to make those changes. I'll never move on if every corner of my place and every focus of my life reminds me of him.

The back door opens, and Annie strolls in, yawning. "Hey, what are you doing here so early?" She loops her handbag over a hook next to mine, then grabs a clean apron. "Well, since you wouldn't tell me what happened with you and Clay last night, maybe you'll tell me this morning before we open up?" She leans her hip against the counter and crosses her arms. Her eyes light up as she observes me. "Let me guess. He kissed you, you liked it, and you freaked out."

I glance at the floor because I'm ashamed of myself. "Yep. He laid his heart on the line, and I pushed him away. But not before—" I feel my face get warm and I can't look up. "Just the taste of his lips, the touch of his hand against my skin— he makes me feel alive again, Annie. Any smart woman would jump at the chance to be with him, but I can't."

"How did he react when you pushed him away?"

I let out a long sigh and push my crazy hair out of my face. "Exactly the way you'd think. He was disappointed, but he walked away like a gentleman. He shouldn't have to beg me to give him a chance."

Annie nods. "You're right. He shouldn't. I was hoping this would end up differently, but I'm not you."

"You aren't the only one disappointed. I'm frustrated and exhausted by the constant guilt and conflicting emotions." I sigh. "It's not all bad though. When I got home, I went through all of Liam's things and put them in boxes. I'll send some to his parents and donate the rest. Of course, I'll keep the important things. I keep asking myself why I had to lose his ring. Did I do it on purpose? Was my subconscious pushing me to let go?

"What if I find it—will I have the inner strength to put it *and mine* in my jewelry box and leave them there?" My heart stops. "Omigod, Annie. Right before I left the beach, I asked Liam to give me a sign that it's okay to move on. You know what happened after that?"

Annie pushes off the counter, her eyes wide. "You saw Clay."

A groan escapes me and I nod.

7

CLAY

I t's been two days since I had an addicting taste of Corinna, felt her warm, gorgeous body against mine. For a short moment, everything was perfect. My future with her was within grasp. I finally had her in my arms, kissing with burning heat and passion. And then she was gone, and the dream became a nightmare. How can I go on now that I had a glimpse and taste of how we could be together?

I've been tempted to go to the café to check up on her but I haven't done it. Begging Corinna to give me her heart is not my style. I've made my feelings clear. If she wants to see me, she'll have to come to me.

But then, Mom and I had a long conversation yesterday. She tried to help me understand what it's like to lose your significant other. Her experience was different—she was devastated when dad died, but it was a relief, too, because he had been suffering so badly. They were married over thirty years. Corinna had no warning. She and Liam didn't even get the chance to start their lives together. They made plans, and they were taken away from them. Mom helped me imagine the pain and even guilt Corinna must be feeling.

I'm the first man she's let into her life since Liam died. It's up to me if I want to walk away or be patient every time she pushes me away.

For her, I'll try to be patient. But I'm going to leave the ball in her court.

My phone rings and I look to see who it is: Mom. I swipe the screen. "Hey, Mom. I can't talk too long; I have a lesson in fifteen."

"No worries. I'll make this short. Do you have time tonight around six?"

"To do what?" My student arrives and I wave as he approaches.

"I forgot to tell you that I found a man's wedding band on the beach the other day. Beautiful ring. Right at the spot I went to after we ate lunch at that Sunshine Café."

"Really? That's pretty cool. Did you post a picture in that Facebook group?"

"Yes, and I found the person who lost it. It's a miracle," she exclaims. "You should have heard how happy they were."

"Great job, Mom. What does that have to do with me?"

"I agreed to meet the owner tonight where I found the ring, but I forgot I had a Pilates class. Last week's was canceled and I don't want to miss two weeks in a row."

"Now we don't want that. I know how you get." I chuckle.

"Smart man. Anyway, would you be able to deliver it for me? I wouldn't trust anybody else because this ring is precious to the one who lost it."

I look at my calendar. I'm free after five. "Sure. No problem. Just text me the details and I'll pick it up later."

"Will do. Thanks for your help. Have fun."

Hours later, I'm almost to the meeting point when my phone dings with a text.

Mom: Hi, Clay. I forgot to tell you the owner will have the matching ring with them. You need to check that the engraving inside matches the other. I'm off to my class. Love you.

I lean against the lamppost where I'm supposed to meet the guy. Mom packed the ring in a box in a little gift bag. It looks like she's bought this person a present instead of just returning a ring. I take the box out of the bag and open it. It is a nice one. Not my style, though. Then again, I've never thought about it.

I pull the ring out of the box and look inside to see how it's engraved.

June 8, 2019 Liam & Corinna September 21, 2019

My stomach bottoms out and I push off the post, searching for Corinna.

8

CORINNA

"Corinna, come here! Quick!" Annie says in that high-pitched voice she only uses when she's really excited.

I rush to the kitchen to find her staring at her phone. "What's going on?"

"Someone found Liam's ring! I just got off the phone with them."

"Holy shit! Really? I can't believe it!" Doubt kicks in. "Are you sure? Do you have a picture of it? I don't want to go meet some psycho who doesn't even have it."

She opens her text messages to the picture and hands me the phone. "The Treasure Hunter found it right where you thought you dropped it on the beach. How crazy is that? She finds everything."

"Why didn't you have me contact her?"

She shrugs. "I wanted to make sure it was the real thing before I got you all excited and then it was a scammer."

"So when do I get to pick it up or what did you agree to?"

"She said she'll meet you at six by the big streetlamp where you enter the beach at the end of Ocean View. Make sure you have your ring with you so you can show her that they match."

I glance at my watch. "That's in a couple of hours." *Ugh. That feels like an eternity.* "What's her name?"

"She said to just call her the Treasure Hunter."

My heart's in my throat. Tears swim in my eyes and I realize I'm smiling. The weight on my heart is gone. But there's something else, too, that I can't pinpoint.

Annie looks at me sternly, and my smile fades away. "When you get that ring back, you are going to put both of them together in a secure place. No more carrying them around. This is your chance for closure."

"I don't—"

She raises her hand. "Nope. You can do this. Save yourself. You have memories of Liam, and they'll never fade. He was a big chapter in your life. Let yourself experience new things now." She grabs my hands and squeezes them tightly. "Promise me you'll try to have an open mind now. Stop comparing everything and everyone to Liam. *You* have changed since he died. You're not the same person anymore."

I take a deep breath, then exhale. "I can't promise, but I'll try."

"That's better than nothing," she says with a reassuring smile.

I hope there's only one person waiting by the lamppost. My hands are sweating for no good reason. What's with all the nerves? I should be excited that someone found the ring buried in the sand. *Might have found it.* I won't believe it until I have it in my hand.

I still have fifteen minutes, but who cares. Maybe the Treasure Hunter is early, too. I walk slowly along the water and turn my wedding band on my finger. I stop to look at the horizon.

Liam, I hope you can hear me somehow. Thank you for helping me find your ring and giving me peace. If you can see me, you know how distraught I've been. But once I get that ring back, baby, I have to say goodbye. I won't be coming back to this point anymore. I have to stop torturing myself and move on with my life. You'll always be my soulmate and my first true love. My love for you will never fade. You'll always have a piece of my heart. I look forward to the day we meet again. I love you.

I slip the ring off my finger and drop it in the pouch, then turn to head to the lamppost.

Air escapes my lungs. No! It can't be.

Joy bubbles in my chest. Clay is walking toward me. What's he doing here? The huge smile on his face tells me what I need to know.

Liam just gave me closure!

I start to run, tears blurring my vision. "Clay, how did you know I was here?"

He extends his arm and opens his hand to reveal Liam's ring.

I shake my head in disbelief. A lone tear drifts down my cheek. "How could you—I don't understand."

"My mom's the Treasure Hunter. She must've put two and two together, and then she set us up. She told me a man was supposed to pick up the ring. When he wasn't here at six, I peeked and… I saw the inscription." He hands it to me, and I slip it carefully into the pouch along with mine.

"Annie knew then. She's so sneaky." I gaze up at Clay. "I can't describe how happy and relieved I am right now." I hold the pouch to my heart for a moment, then put it deep in my handbag. "It's kind of amazing that you're the one to return it to me. Almost like… a sign."

He inches closer. "Corinna, I don't care how it happened. I just know that we're meant to be. My goal everyday will be to show you how much we belong together. I've loved you from the first moment I saw you. It wasn't our time then, but it is now." He cups the back of my neck, and his lips capture mine possessively, kissing away all my doubts and fears. I melt into him and just enjoy this unforgettable moment.

Clay and Annie have been right all along. I don't need to push Clay away. My feelings scare the hell out of me, but I won't let my fears take over anymore. Liam was my past, and Clay's my future. It's time to live again.

I rake my hand through his wind-blown hair and break this breathtaking kiss. "Thank you for waiting for me."

"I would've waited forever. Thankfully, I don't have to." He leans in for another kiss, and I surrender again. I'll never stop.

When I was young, I used to dream about finding my soulmate. Never in my wildest imagination did I think I'd be blessed with two.

ABOUT THE AUTHOR

Kristina Beck was born and raised in New Jersey, USA, and lived there for thirty years. She later moved to Germany where she lives with her German husband and three children. She is an avid reader of many genres, but romance always takes precedence. She loves everything coffee, wine, dark chocolate, power naps, flowers, eighties movies, and OneRepublic. Her hobbies include writing, reading, fitness, and forever trying to improve her German-language skills.

For more updates on her books, sign up for her newsletter and follower her on social media.

Check out her website!
www.kristinabeck.com

facebook.com/krissybeck73

instagram.com/krissybeck96

amazon.com/author/kristinabeck

bookbub.com/authors/kristina-beck

goodreads.com/kristina_beck

www.ingramcontent.com/pod-product-compliance
Lightning Source LLC
LaVergne TN
LVHW011605210726